The Night Before Christmas

Silver Dolphin

Silver Dolphin Books
An imprint of Printers Row Publishing Group
A division of Readerlink Distribution Services, LLC
9717 Pacific Heights Blvd, San Diego, CA 92121
www.silverdolphinbooks.com

Printers Row Publishing Group is a division of Readerlink Distribution Services, LLC.
Silver Dolphin Books is a registered trademark of Readerlink Distribution Services, LLC.

All notations of errors or omissions should be addressed to Silver Dolphin Books, Editorial Department, at the above address.

ISBN: 978-1-64517-815-6

Manufactured, printed, and assembled in Heshan, China.
Second printing, May 2022. LP/05/22
26 25 24 23 22 2 3 4 5 6

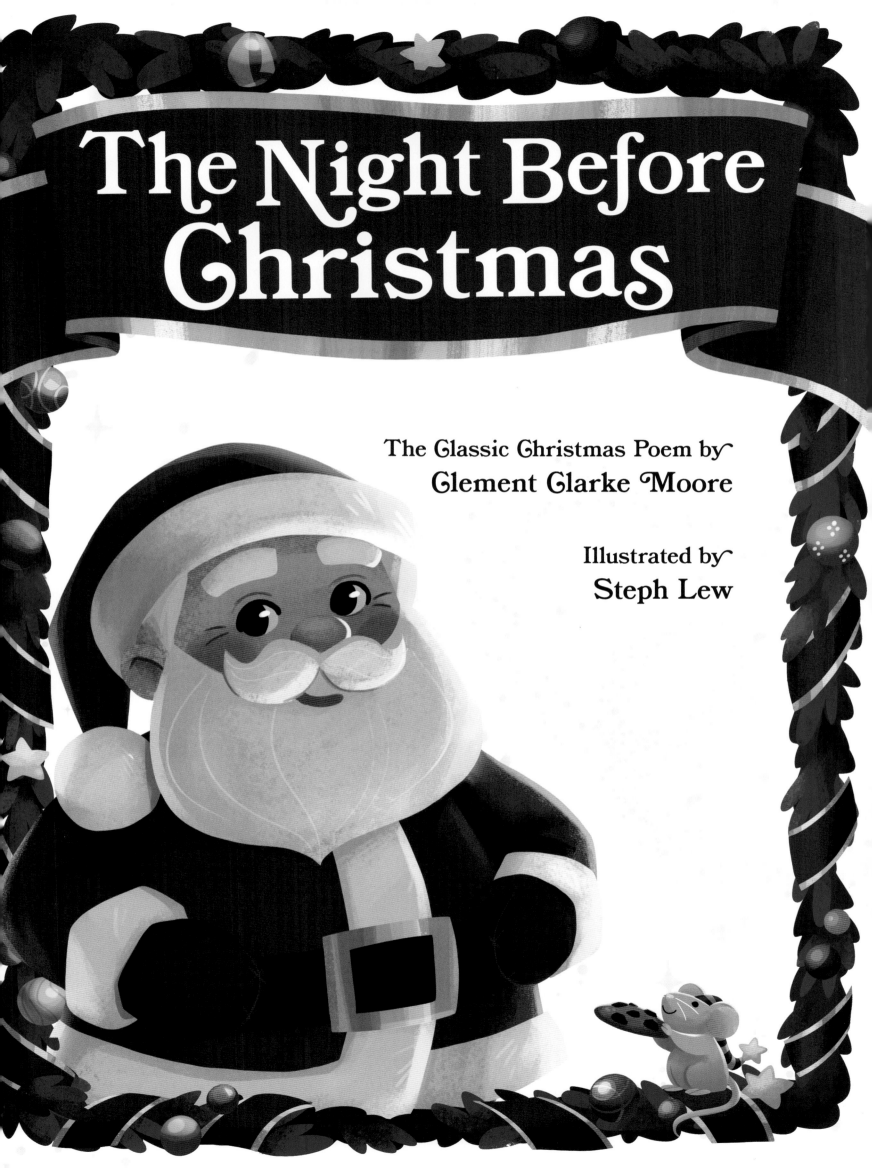

The Night Before Christmas

The Classic Christmas Poem by
Clement Clarke Moore

Illustrated by
Steph Lew

'Twas the night before Christmas,
when all through the house
not a creature was stirring,
not even a mouse.

The stockings were hung
by the chimney with care
in hopes that St. Nicholas
soon would be there.

The children were nestled
all snug in their beds,
while visions of sugarplums
danced in their heads;

And mamma in her kerchief,
and I in my cap,
had just settled down
for a long winter's nap,

When out on the lawn
there arose such a clatter,
I sprang from the bed
to see what was the matter.

Away to the window
I flew like a flash,
tore open the shutters
and threw up the sash.

The moon on the breast
of the new-fallen snow
gave the luster of midday
to objects below,

When, what to my wondering
eyes should appear,
but a miniature sleigh,
and eight tiny reindeer,

With a little old driver,
so lively and quick,
I knew in a moment
it must be St. Nick.

More rapid than eagles
his coursers they came,
and he whistled, and shouted,
and called them by name:

On, *Comet!*
On, *Cupid!*

On, *Donner* and *Blitzen!*

"To the top of the porch!
To the top of the wall!
Now dash away! Dash away!
Dash away all!"

As dry leaves that before
the wild hurricane fly,
when they meet with an obstacle,
mount to the sky;

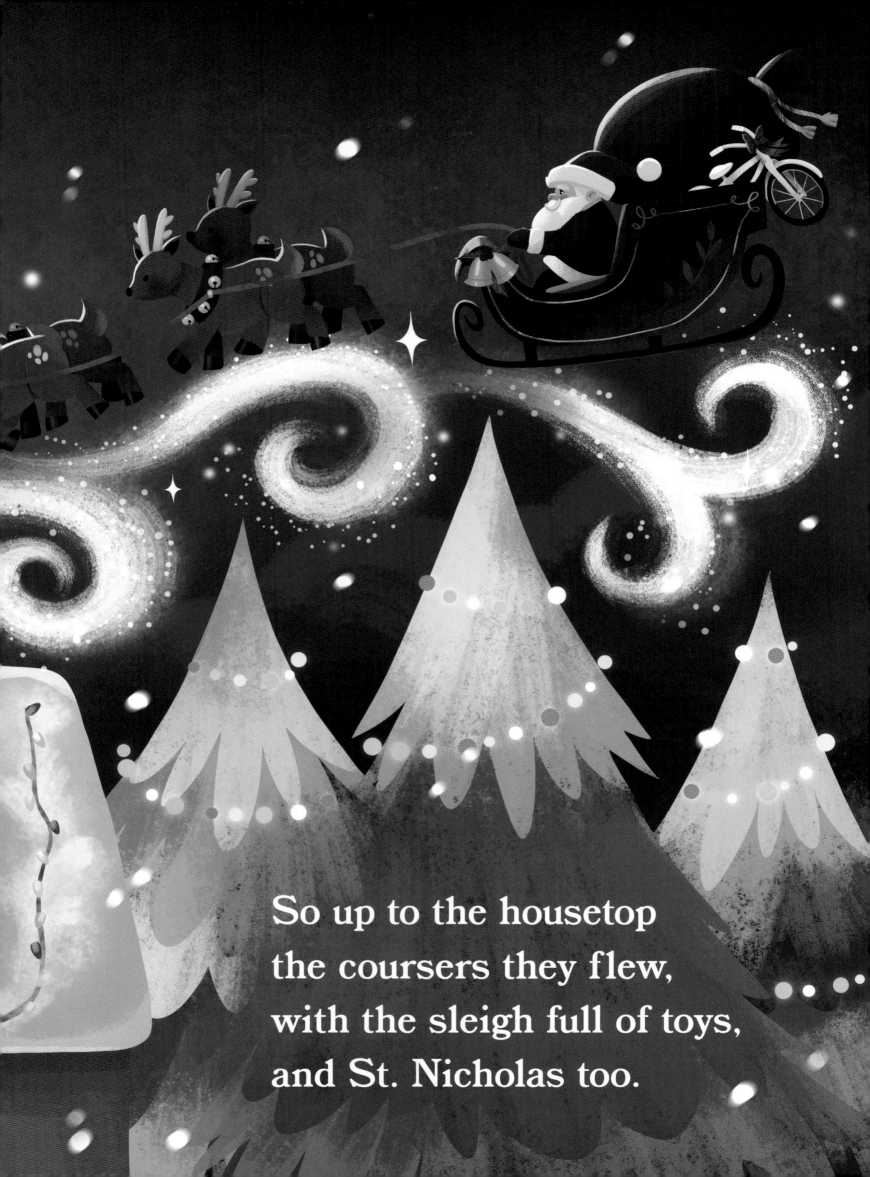

So up to the housetop
the coursers they flew,
with the sleigh full of toys,
and St. Nicholas too.

And then, in a twinkling,
I heard on the roof
the prancing and pawing
of each little hoof.

As I drew in my head,
and was turning around,
down the chimney St. Nicholas
came with a bound.

He was dressed all in fur,
from his head to his foot,
and his clothes were all tarnished
with ashes and soot;

A bundle of toys he had
flung on his back,
and he looked like a peddler
just opening his pack.

His eyes—how they twinkled!
His dimples how merry!
His cheeks were like roses,
his nose like a cherry!

His droll little mouth
was drawn up like a bow,
and the beard of his chin
was as white as the snow.

The stump of a pipe
he held tight in his teeth,
and the smoke it encircled
his head like a wreath;

He had a broad face
and a little round belly,
that shook when he laughed,
like a bowl full of jelly.

He was chubby and plump,
a right jolly old elf,
and I laughed when I saw him,
in spite of myself;

A wink of his eye
and a twist of his head,
soon gave me to know
I had nothing to dread.

He spoke not a word,
but went straight to his work,
and filled all the stockings;
then turned with a jerk,

And laying his finger
aside of his nose,
and giving a nod,
up the chimney he rose.

He sprang to his sleigh,
to his team gave a whistle,
and away they all flew
like the down of a thistle.

But I heard him exclaim,
as he drove out of sight,

"Merry Christmas
to all, and to all
a good night!"

Can you find the little mouse in every scene?